Pig Pig Rides

Pig Pig Rides

by David McPhail

A Unicorn Book • E. P. Dutton   New York

for cousin Mark

Library of Congress Cataloging in Publication Data

McPhail, David M.   Pig Pig rides.
(A Unicorn book)

Summary: Over breakfast, Pig Pig informs his mother
about all the wonderful feats he intends to
accomplish that day, such as jumping 500 elephants
on his motorcycle and driving a rocket to the moon.
[1. Pigs—Fiction] I. Title.
PZ7.M2427Pk 1982 [E] 82-9777
ISBN 0-525-44024-0   AACR2

Published in the United States by E. P. Dutton,
a division of Penguin Books USA Inc.

Editor: Emilie McLeod   Designer: Isabel Warren-Lynch

Printed in Hong Kong by South China Printing Co.
First Edition
10 9 8 7 6 5

Pig Pig and his mother were eating breakfast.

"What are you doing today?" asked Pig Pig's mother.

"Well," said Pig Pig,

"I've got some stuff to deliver."

"That's nice," said his mother.

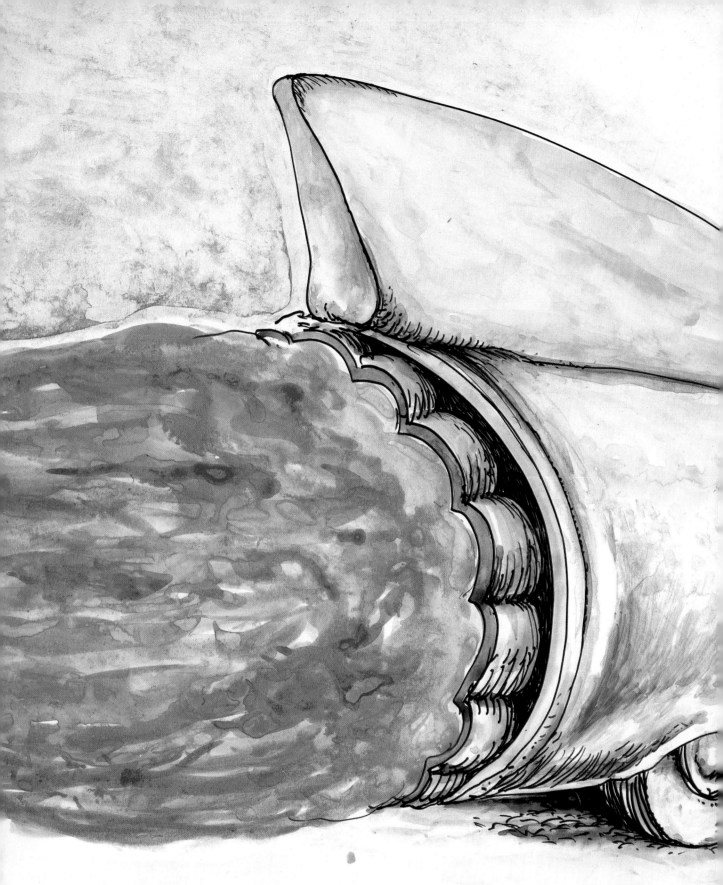

"Then I'll take my racing car and try for a speed record."

"Ummm," said his mother.

"I'll jump 500 elephants on my motorcycle."

"And then?" said his mother.

"Then I'll race my horse at Rocking Ham Park!"

"Oh?" said his mother.

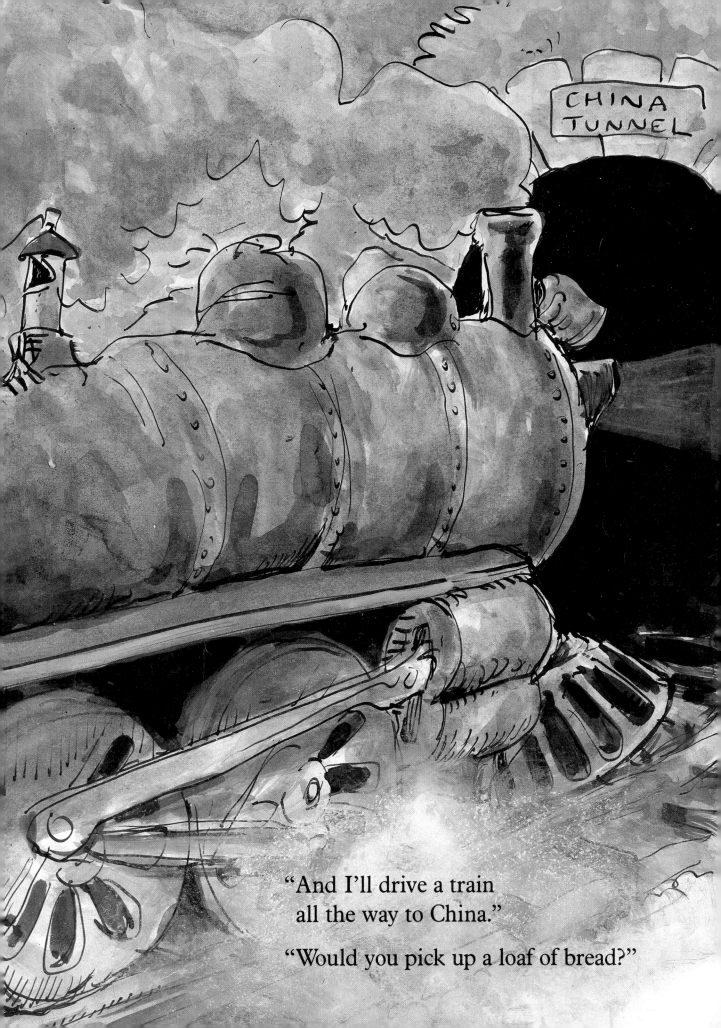

"And I'll drive a train
all the way to China."

"Would you pick up a loaf of bread?"

"And when I'm back, I might even drive a rocket
to the moon. I'm off!" said Pig Pig.

"You will be back before dark?"

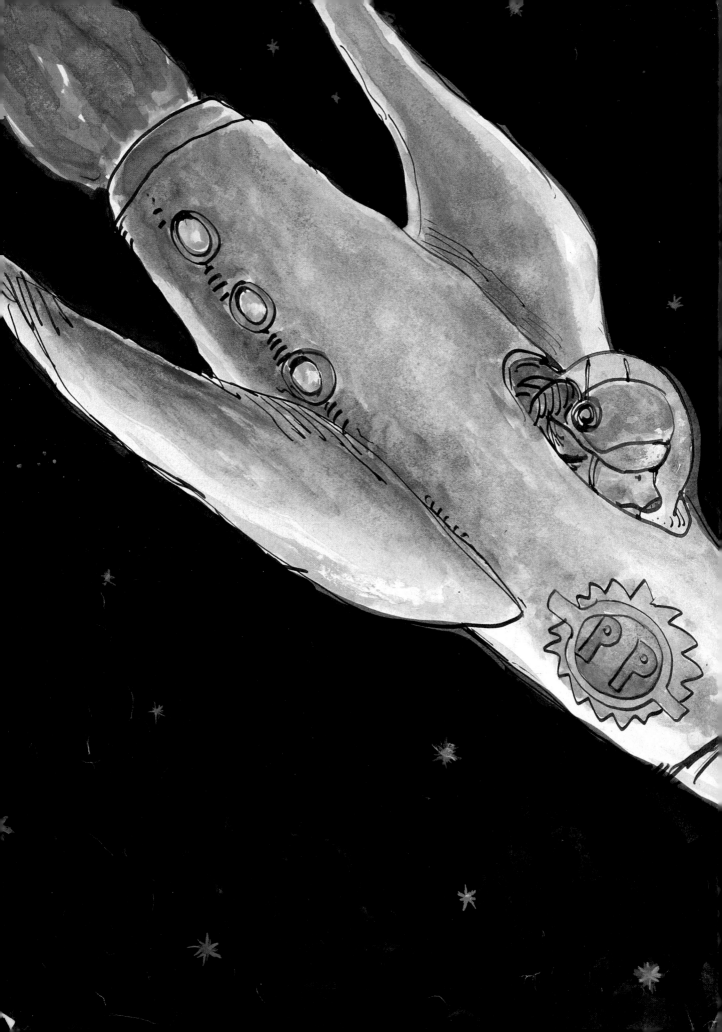

"Please be careful."

"Why?" asked Pig Pig.

"Because I love you," said his mother.